This is Albert the bear. Even from the back he looks sad. His head hangs low. His shoulders are hunched. His arms flop loosely by his sides.

From the front, Albert the bear looks very sad indeed. He has the saddest eyes you ever saw. Which is strange, because Albert. . . . But wait. Let's tell his story from the very beginning.

Albert the Bear

Copyright © 2002 by Nick Butterworth

Printed in Hong Kong. All rights reserved.

www.harperchildrens.com

Library of Congress Cataloging-in-Publication Data is available.

First U.S. edition, HarperCollins Publishers, Inc., 2003

Originally published in Great Britain by HarperCollins Publishers Ltd., 2002

1 2 3 4 5 6 7 8 9 10

❖

First Edition

Albert the Bear

Nick Butterworth

HarperCollins_Publishers_

When Albert the bear first appeared in
Mr. Jolly's toy shop, the other toys could
only stare. He looked so sad.

"Poor love," said Sally the hippo. "We must
try to cheer him up."

"You could do your funny dancing," said Toby the cat. "That would make him laugh."

"My dancing is not funny," said Sally. "It is beautiful and artistic." The other toys tried not to smile.

"I know a joke," said a little mouse called Pickle. "But I can't remember the funny bit at the end."

Everyone agreed that this could make the joke a lot less funny.

Then Jack-in-a-box had an idea. "Why don't we all try very hard to think of something happy and funny. Something to cheer up a very sad bear. Then we could put everything together. . .

and make a show!"

It was a good idea. Everybody thought so. The toys sat quietly thinking. What could they say? What could they do?

Maurice the steam engine let off a little steam as he tried to think. Lizzie the humming top hummed to herself as she thought. Hmmmmmmm. . . .

"I've remembered my joke!" squeaked Pickle suddenly.

"Sssh! dear," said Sally. "I'm getting an idea."

All at once, it seemed that the other toys were getting ideas too.

Toby began to smile, and Jack-in-a-box started to chuckle. Sally began to titter and went to find some face paints.

Albert the bear watched as the toys became very busy. What was going on? What were they up to?

A lbert did not have to wait very long to find out. Sally was the first to introduce herself.

"Good evening!" she said with a bow. "I am Sally, hippopotamus and ballerina. This evening, we, the toys of Mr. Jolly's toy shop, will present a Happy and Entertaining Treat, to Cheer, Amuse, and Tickle the Funny Bone of a Very Sad Bear."

Albert looked puzzled.

"I am very pleased to meet you," he said. "I am Albert the bear. But, please . . . you must not think that I am—"

"Silence, please, for Miss Pickle!" the hippopotamus boomed loudly. Pickle stood nervously in front of Albert. She shuffled her feet and cleared her throat. But no words came. Whatever Pickle had remembered earlier, she had suddenly forgotten again.

"I can't remember my joke," she said miserably.

"Never mind," said Albert kindly. "I am sure it was very funny. And you really must not think that I am—"

But at that moment, with a twang and a zing, Jack-in-a-box sprang out of his box. He bounced up and down in front of Albert and began to sing.

"I bounce . . . with a BOING!
I bounce . . . with a POING!
And while . . . I am bouncing,
I'm singing . . . this SOING!"

"Be careful, dear," said Sally. But Jack was enjoying himself. He bounced even higher.

"I like . . . to bounce HIGH!
As high . . . as the SKY!
Sometimes . . . when I'm bouncing,
I'm sure . . . I could FL—"

THUMP!

Poor Jack. He bounced so high, he bumped his head on a shelf and fell in a tangled heap in front of Albert.

"Slight technical problem," mumbled Jack as he tried to untie the knot that he had accidentally tied in his long body.

Albert hid his face in his paws.

"Please do not worry," he said. "You really, really must not think that I am—"

Once again, Sally did not let him finish. To Albert's amazement, she leaped out in front of him, wearing a yellow, pointed hat and a big, red smile.

Of course, Sally did mean to be funny. But she didn't mean to slip. Or slide. And she most certainly didn't mean to crash into Albert. But that is just what Sally did.

The bear and the hippopotamus
landed together in a confused heap. From
underneath Sally, Albert let out a great roar.

"PLEASE!" he shouted. "I keep trying to tell you! I AM NOT UNHAPPY!" There was silence. As Sally and Albert struggled to get up, Albert went on, "I am not sad at all. It is just the way I am made. I just happen to have a sad look on my face."

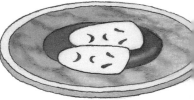

"Oh, no you don't!" interrupted Toby the cat. "Not anymore!"

Suddenly everyone saw that Albert the bear was wearing a great, big, red smile! It was Sally's smile.

"Oh! Silly me," said Sally. "I'm so sorry. I must have kissed you by mistake!"

The toys began to laugh. But what was happening to Albert?

His shoulders began to shake, and he grabbed hold of his tummy. His nose wrinkled up, and his sad eyes almost disappeared.

Then, to everyone's great surprise, Albert the bear roared out the funniest and the loudest laugh any of the toys had ever heard.

"H-HEE! H-HEE! H-HEE!"

Albert's enormous laugh made everyone else laugh even more.

"H-HEE! H-HEE! H-HEE! H-HEE!"

"Well," Jack-in-a-box giggled,
"who would have thought
that a little kiss could put such a
big smile on someone's face!"
Everybody laughed again.
But the biggest, deepest, loudest,
and funniest laugh of all
came from a sad-looking
bear called . . .
Albert.

A big thank you!

Some familiar faces make guest appearances in this book with the permission of:

Mick Inkpen, for Kipper; Chorion plc, for Noddy;
Martin Handford, for Where's Waldo?; Jane Hissey, for Old Bear and Little Bear;
David McKee, for Elmer; Michael Bond, for Paddington;
Raymond Briggs, for The Snowman; HIT Entertainment plc, for Bob the Builder.
Percy the Park Keeper's friend, the fox, appeared without anyone's permission.
Q Pootle 5 just appeared out of the blue.